The Outfoxed Fox

Based on a Japanese Kyogen

By **Tim Myers**
Illustrated by **Ariel Ya-Wen Pang**

Marshall Cavendish Children

Marshall Cavendish Corporation, 99 White Plains Road, Tarrytown, NY 10591
www.marshallcavendish.us/kids

Library of Congress Cataloging-in-Publication Data
Myers, Tim (Tim Brian)
The outfoxed fox / by Tim Myers ; illustrated by Ariel Ya-Wen Pang.
p. cm.
Summary: A proud old fox scorns a youngster's simple plan for stopping the hunter who has grown skillful at kiling foxes, but when he sets out to handle the problem himself, he runs into trouble
Includes facts about kyogen, a traditional type of Japanese drama, and the play from which this story is derived.
ISBN 978-0-7614-5356-7
[1. Fables. 2. Foxes—Fiction. 3. Simplicity—Fiction. 4. Hunting—Fiction.] I. Pang, Ariel, ill. II. Title.
PZ8.2.M8997Out 2007
[E]—dc22
2006030234

The text of this book is set in Minion.
The illustrations were rendered in mixed media, including pencil, watercolor, oil paint, and color pencil.

Book design by Vera Soki
Editor: Margery Cuyler

Printed in Malaysia
First edition
1 3 5 6 4 2
Marshall Cavendish
Children

HUNDREDS OF YEARS AGO, in the mountains of Japan, there lived a hunter who'd grown very skillful at catching foxes. The country people shook their heads at this, knowing that foxes were cunning and possessed great magic, often turning into humans or other animals to get what they wanted. Some even said that an especially clever fox could take on the appearance of a god.

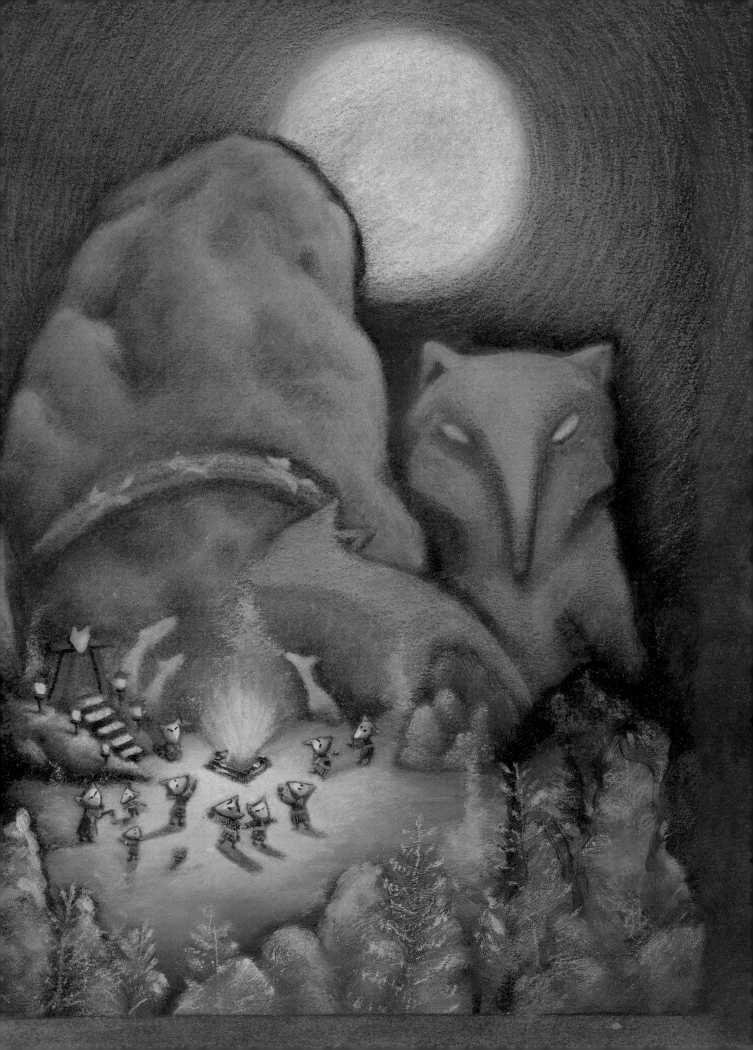

But the hunter ignored this talk and went on trapping foxes. Finally he'd caught so many that the foxes realized something would have to be done.

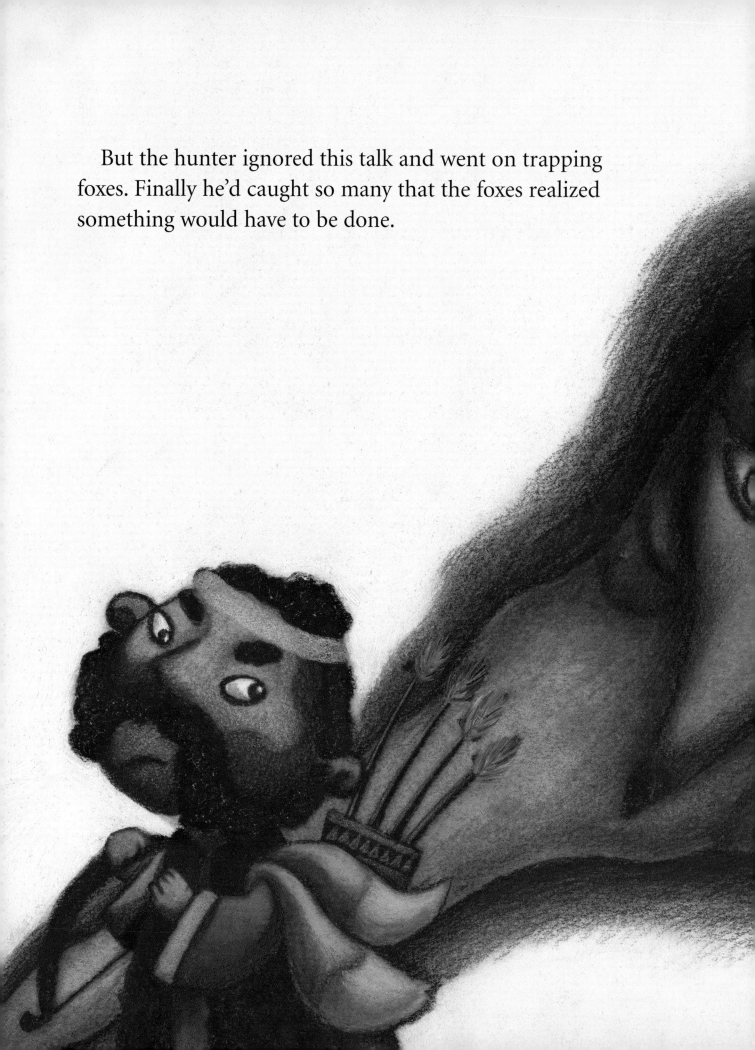

One day the head of the local fox family called all his kin together to discuss the matter.

Sitting on his haunches beside a mountain stream, the old fox addressed the circle of foxes around him.

"I tell you, we must do something!" he shouted. "Unless we stop this hunter, he's likely to destroy us all! Now—who has an idea?"

All the foxes were silent. They knew the bossy old fox was only pretending to be interested in their ideas; as always, he already knew what he wanted to do. A wind stirred snow dust down from the pine branches above them. But then, to everyone's surprise, a young fox with crooked whiskers spoke up in a quiet voice.

"Maybe one of us could go to him as the ghost
of a fox, and haunt him till he understands that
he must stop killing."

The proud old fox was angry that this youngster would even dare make a suggestion. "What a pitiful idea!" he mocked. "Did you just say the first thing that came into your head? That would never work—and do you know why? It's too simple!"

The young fox just hung his head.

The old fox looked around at the others. "I have a much better plan," he said grandly. "In the morning I shall turn myself into the hunter's uncle, the old priest Hakuzosu. Then I shall go to the hunter and convince him to stop trapping foxes. With my vast intelligence, I'm bound to persuade him! And he'll listen to a priest. Unlike *some* of us"—here he glared at the young fox—"the hunter has proper respect for his elders."

So the next morning the old fox woke up, stretched a bit, and came up out of his den. With a twinkling of sunlight through wind-blown snow, he changed himself into the priest. Then he traveled down the mountain and was soon sitting in the hunter's house, drinking tea and warming himself at the hibachi.

"Nephew," the old fox-priest began, "people tell me you've been killing foxes."

The hunter looked surprised. "Oh no, venerable Uncle!" he lied. "Our Lord Buddha has forbidden the taking of life!"

Suddenly a dog barked from a nearby farm, and the startled fox-priest leapt to his feet, looking around wildly. Then he remembered he was supposed to act like a human, and sat back down again.

"I'm sorry to jump up like that, Nephew. It's just that I thought I might be sitting on my tail—my teacup, I mean! Do go on."

The young hunter continued. "As I was saying, Uncle—I don't trap foxes."

But when the old fox kept asking, the hunter eventually admitted the truth, adding that he sold the fox skins.

"I'm saddened to hear this!" the old fox said, making his human face look stern. "You must give up this sinful behavior! Besides, foxes are highly intelligent beings, and they don't easily forget crimes against their own kind."

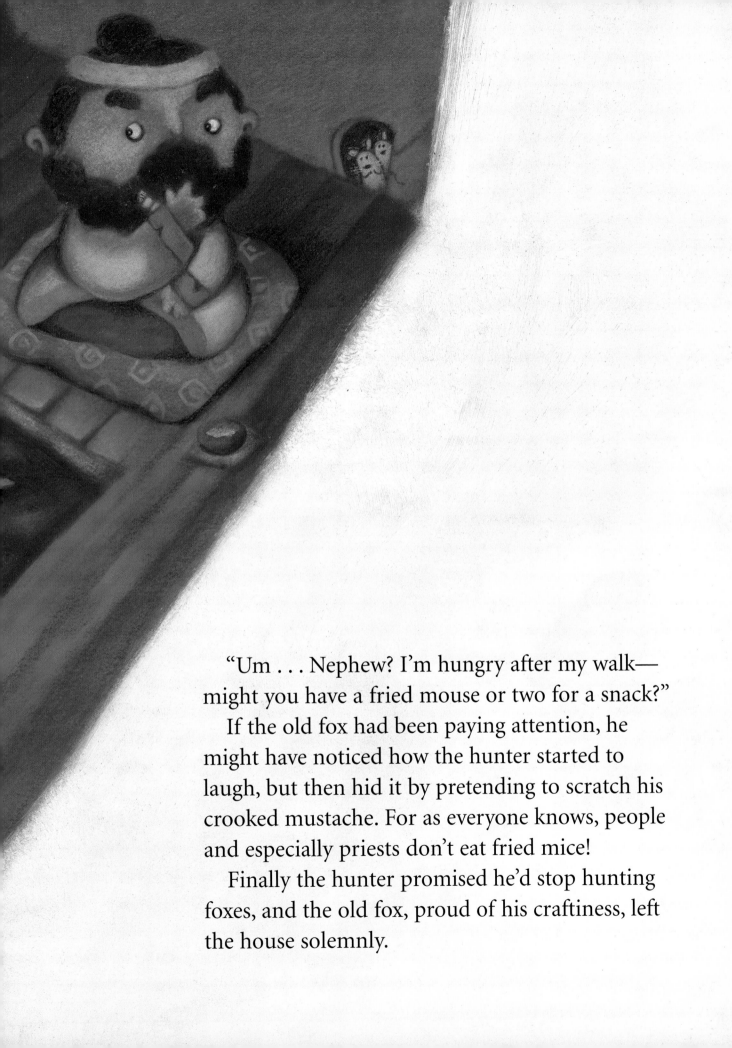

"Um . . . Nephew? I'm hungry after my walk—
might you have a fried mouse or two for a snack?"

If the old fox had been paying attention, he
might have noticed how the hunter started to
laugh, but then hid it by pretending to scratch his
crooked mustache. For as everyone knows, people
and especially priests don't eat fried mice!

Finally the hunter promised he'd stop hunting
foxes, and the old fox, proud of his craftiness, left
the house solemnly.

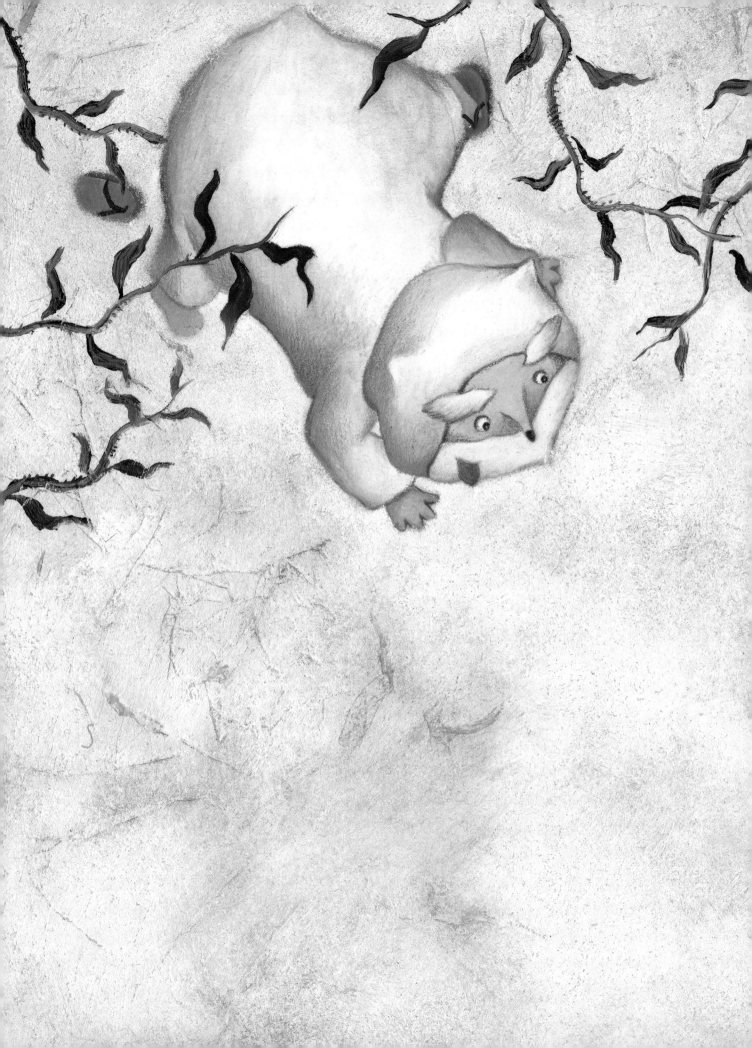

As the old fox walked back toward the mountains, still in human form, he noticed a delicious smell coming from some low bushes beside the path. Getting down on all fours, he sniffed about and quickly found a perfectly ripe persimmon lying in the snow. Its orange reddish skin made his mouth water. He didn't stop to wonder why it was there, and in the middle of winter besides!

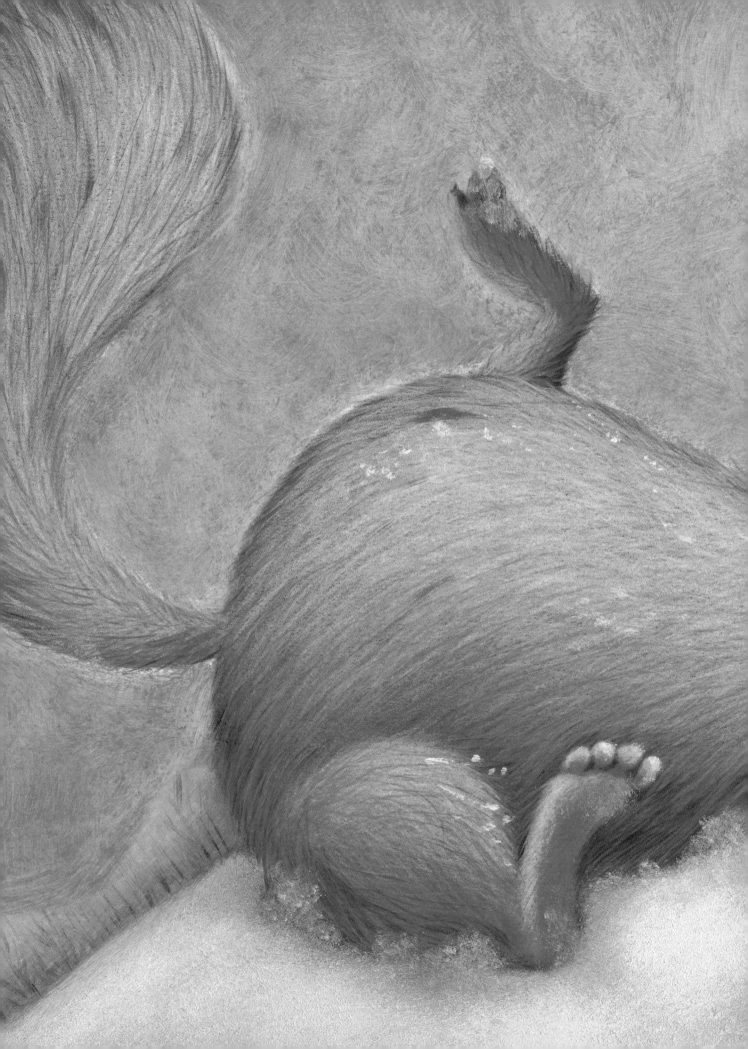

The moment he touched it, a hidden snare snapped onto his hand—he was caught fast! This surprised him so much that he instantly lost all his magical concentration. Suddenly there was no priest at all—only a terrified old fox with one paw caught in a trap.

After a time he heard the sound he'd feared most—the footsteps of a human coming through the snow. Soon the hunter was standing over him.

"So, old fox, you thought you could trick me by pretending to be my uncle? That was a foolish thing to do!"

The old fox cowered, certain his end was near.

"You know why your trick didn't work, fox?" the hunter shouted.

The old fox shook his head miserably.

"It wasn't *simple* enough!"

Suddenly everything was quiet. When the old fox looked up, the hunter wasn't there. In his place stood the young fox with the crooked whiskers.

"Here—let me help you out of that trap," the young fox said with a smile, unfastening the snare.

"You!" the old fox gasped. "You . . . turned yourself into the *hunter*! It was *you* I was talking to all along!"

"That's right," the young fox answered casually.

"But where's the real hunter?"

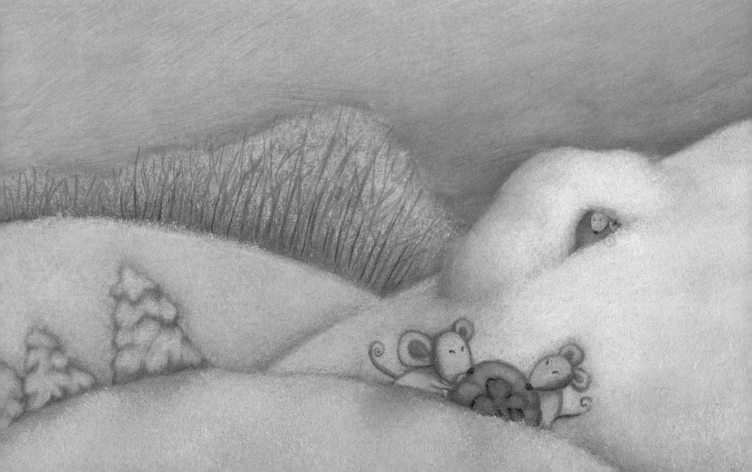

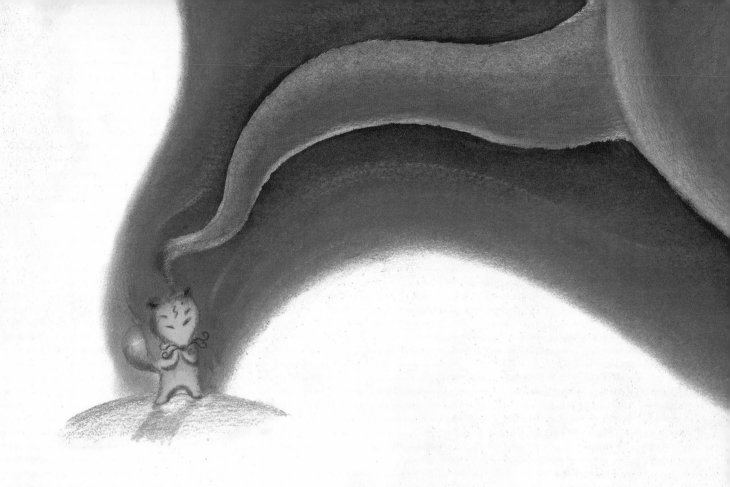

"Last night I came on my own and appeared to him as a fox-ghost. He felt so guilty and remorseful that he packed up and left early this morning. That's one hunter who won't be killing any more foxes!"

For a moment the old fox was speechless. Then he said quietly, "I suppose sometimes simple *is* best."

As they began walking back toward their home in the mountains, the young fox couldn't resist enjoying his success just one more time.

"By the way," he said in a sly voice, "I'm rather hungry after all that magic. . . . Might you have a fried mouse or two for a snack?"

The old fox just hung his head.

AUTHOR'S NOTE

This story is my version of "Tsurigitsune" ("Fox Trapping"), a traditional Japanese *kyogen*. The Japanese drama called *noh* is famous, and very serious—it relies heavily on music, is profoundly aesthetic, addresses deep themes, and is sometimes presented in daylong programs. *Kyogen*, by contrast, are lighter, often farcical, and more colloquial and realistic; they're usually staged as interludes during longer *noh* performances. The *kyogen* form (the name can be translated as "mad words") is believed to have evolved from a kind of dance called *sarugaku* or "monkey music."

But *kyogen* is just as traditional as *noh*, and it became widely popular during the Muromachi Period (AD 1380–1466). About 200 traditional *kyogen* are still performed. But, as one expert says, "Not even a single name is left to us of those who composed" these wonderful plays.

My version of "Tsurigitsune" expands the traditional story. But I've kept the basic plot and the central themes. I love how this story presents the reality of our human desire for both psychological and egotistical satisfaction but reminds us through comedy that such desire can sometimes lead us astray. I also love how its satire is balanced by a higher moral calling: the Buddhist belief in nonviolence toward all sentient beings.

—T. M.